Written by
Veronica Wagner

Illustrated by
Art Mawhinney
and the Disney Storybook Art Team

Book design by Pamela Seatter

Published by Phoenix International Publications, Inc.
8501 West Higgins Road   59 Gloucester Place
Chicago, Illinois 60631   London W1U 8JJ

www.pikidsmedia.com

Printed in Canada.
p i kids is a trademark of Phoenix International Publications, Inc.,
and is registered in the United States.
Look and Find is a trademark of Phoenix International Publications, Inc.,
and is registered in the United States and Canada.

8 7 6 5 4 3 2 1

ISBN: 978-1-5037-2503-4

DISNEY
TSUM TSUM

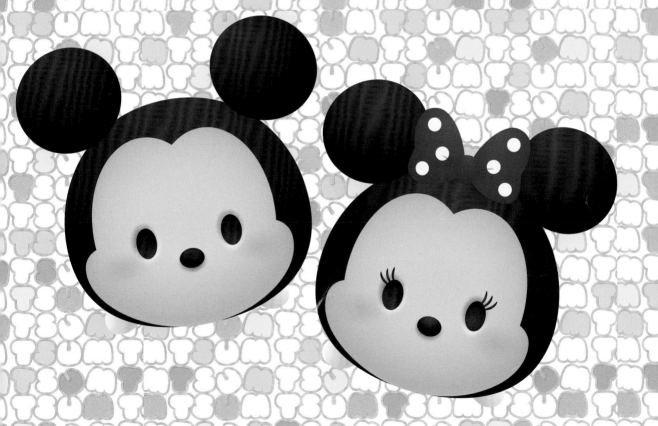

Look and Find®

pi kids® Phoenix International Publications, Inc.

Chicago • London • New York • Hamburg • Mexico City • Paris • Sydney

What *are* Disney Tsum Tsum?
In Japanese, tsum tsum means "stack stack."
And that's just what Disney Tsum Tsum do.
Any time. Any way. Anywhere.

Whatever one Disney Tsum Tsum can't do alone,
a stack stack can handle with ease!

Disney Tsum Tsum come together from different worlds and stories...to make one big, happy family.

Can you find one Disney Tsum Tsum in each of these five stacks whose origin is different from the others?

These Disney Tsum Tsum are special pals. Can you spot this happy pair—everywhere? They're stacked together in each spread of the book.

Each Disney Tsum Tsum
    plays a part
To make their stacks
    a work of art.

Find all six Dumbos
    in this scene.
They're hiding there,
    betwixt, between:

Robot arms
   are awfully handy
For dunking things
   in chocolate candy!

Look left, look right,
   look up, look down.
Find these six pals,
   all cocoa crowned.

Daisy Duck

Pluto

Minnie Mouse

Eeyore

Chip

Tigger

These friends love
to watch the fish.
Marie? She thinks
they look delish.

Do Disney Tsum Tsum
like to swim?
Find these six
who've jumped right in!

Curious Oyster

Mike

Cleo

Donald Duck

Piglet

Alien

Are these two pictures just the same?
No, they're not, and that's the game.

Take a look! Be sharp. Be wary.
Find the ten ways that they vary.

April showers
bring May flowers
And some growing
stack-stack towers.

Disney Tsum Tsum
like the sun!
Find these six
before you're done:

Dale

Tinkerbell

Bambi

Patch

Chip

Thumper

Fireworks boom
    and burst and shimmer—
Disney Tsum Tsum
    shine and glimmer!

Spinning in
    their sky gyrations,
Can you spot
    these friends' formations?

Clock gears turn
    with a tickity-tock
As stack-stacks build
    inside the clock!

In among
    the springs and wheels,
Disney Tsum Tsum
    are revealed:

Tigger

Seven
Dwarfs

Sulley

Pluto

Jiminy
Cricket

Mickey
Mouse

Here's the latest stacking craze: lining up to make a maze.

Now trace a path—it could be tricky!
Help Minnie find her way to Mickey.

You're entering match-up territory.
Find pairs of pals from the same story.

Find eighteen pairs, like Mike and Boo.
It's fun (though a bit tricky too)!

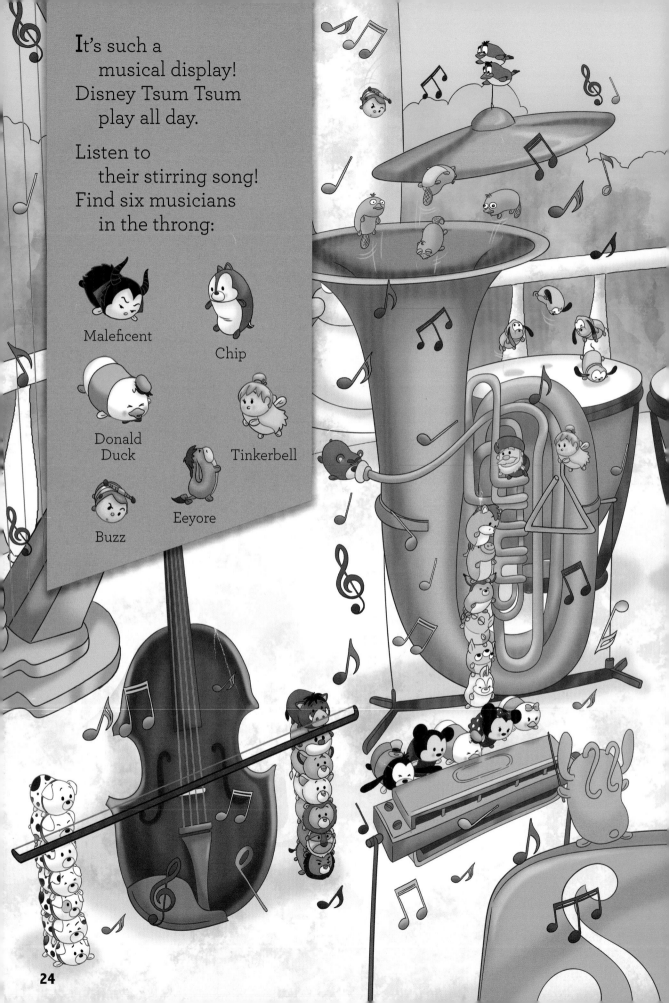

It's such a
  musical display!
Disney Tsum Tsum
  play all day.

Listen to
  their stirring song!
Find six musicians
  in the throng:

Maleficent

Chip

Donald
Duck

Tinkerbell

Buzz

Eeyore

Decorating
Minnie's cake
Is one huge task
to undertake!

If you search,
and stare, and peer,
You'll find these bakers
working here:

Snow White

Piglet

Figaro

this Dumbo

Winnie the Pooh

Cheshire Cat

Disney Tsum Tsum
think the fair
Is a day of fun
beyond compare!

Playing, riding,
munching snacks—
Find these six
in fairground stacks:

Lady and Tramp

Alice and
White Rabbit

Pluto and Goofy

Chip and Dale

Daisy and
Donald Duck

Buzz and Woody

FUN WHEEL

Lucky Duck

DRINK ME

Memorize this stack of ten.
Will you know it, seen again?

These travelers know
   it's never boring
To head on out
   and go exploring.

North, south,
   east, and west,
These pals are on
   a temple quest:

Perry

Tigger

Scrump

Jessie

Pinocchio

Don

Underneath the flashing lights, Groovy dancers are a sight!

Listen to that music mix! Can you spot the Disco Six?

Happy

Maleficent

Snow White

Alice

Goofy

Prospector Pete

From their seats,
    fans watch and cheer.
Will their team
    win big this year?

On and off
    the half-time field,
These six champions
    are concealed:

Doc

Goofy

Alice

Minnie Mouse

this Dumbo

this
Donald Duck

Answer Key

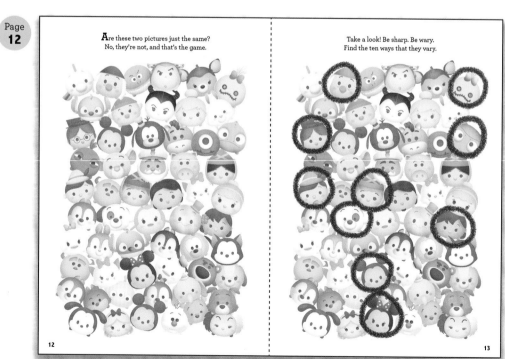

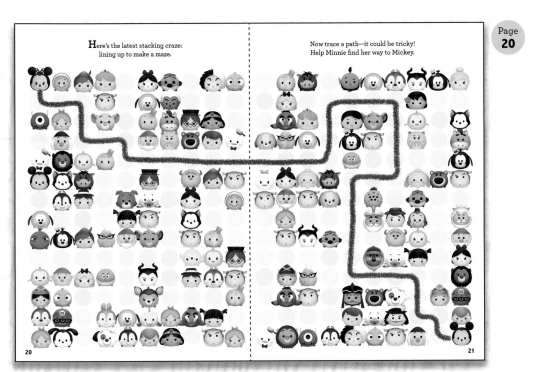

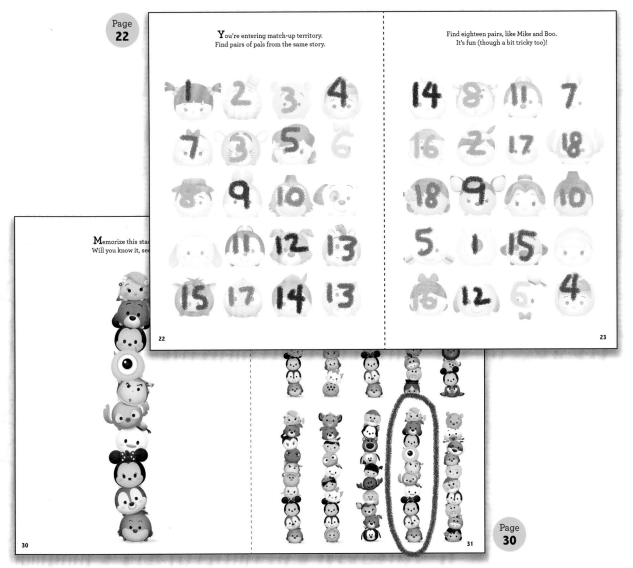

Here's the latest stacking craze:
lining up to make a maze.

Now trace a path—it could be tricky!
Help Minnie find her way to Mickey.

20

21

You're entering match-up territory.
Find pairs of pals from the same story.

Find eighteen pairs, like Mike and Boo.
It's fun (though a bit tricky too)!

22

23

Memorize this stac
Will you know it, see

30

31

Ah, the things Disney Tsum Tsum do for their art! Spot these artists and art supplies in the studio:

purple paintball

this paint tube

Stitch

palette

pink eraser

Winnie the Pooh

Page 6

Page 10

Chocolate is SWEET... especially when you add these flavors to savor. Can you find them in the factory?

coconut

coffee

orange

cherries

peanut butter

peppermint stick

Page 8

Page 14

Bubble, bubble, on the double! Search for three things that are better dry than wet...

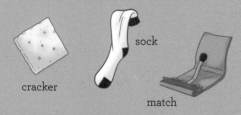

sock

cracker

match

...and three things that are more useful wet than dry:

umbrella

mop

squirt gun

Bugs like gardens too! Beetle on back to the flowerbed to find these insect inhabitants:

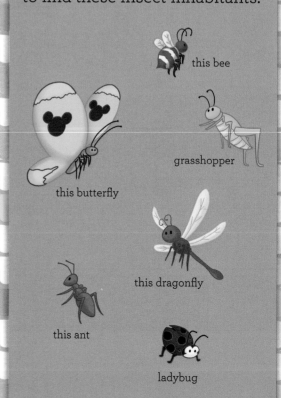

this bee

grasshopper

this butterfly

this dragonfly

this ant

ladybug

Pop! Bang! Zip! Rocket back to the fireworks to find these other nighttime lights:

torch

flashlight

hurricane lamp

magma lamp

candle

firefly

Page 16

Page 24

You can't tell time without numbers! Can you find the numerals 1 to 12 inside the clock?

Page 18

Page 26

Turn back to the bandstand to take note of these notes. Can you spot them all?

It's berry sweet of the Disney Tsum Tsum to make a cake for Minnie! Can you find these flavorsome fruits on the table?

white raspberry

black blackberry

this red strawberry

green gooseberry

orange cloudberry

this blue blueberry

These fair foods are fair game! Canter back to the carnival and spot them all:

pickle on a stick

corn on the cob

corn dog

cream puff

caramel apple

this doughnut

Page 28

Page 34

While the Disney Tsum Tsum keep an eye on the temple's treasure, the local inhabitants are keeping tabs on *them*. Turn back to the temple to find these studious sentinels:

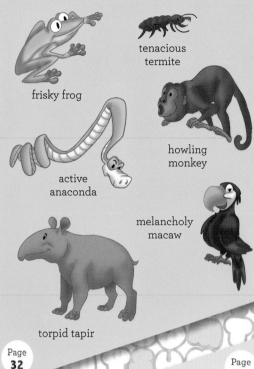

frisky frog

tenacious termite

howling monkey

active anaconda

melancholy macaw

torpid tapir

Page 32

Page 36

Can you dig these disco doo-dads? Hustle back to the dance floor to find them under the mirror ball:

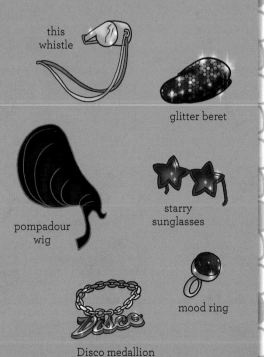

this whistle

glitter beret

pompadour wig

starry sunglasses

Disco medallion

mood ring

Play ball! Go back to the game to spot these sporty spheres:

beach ball

bowling ball

baseball

this croquet ball

football

this soccer ball